This **Picture Mammoth** *belongs to*

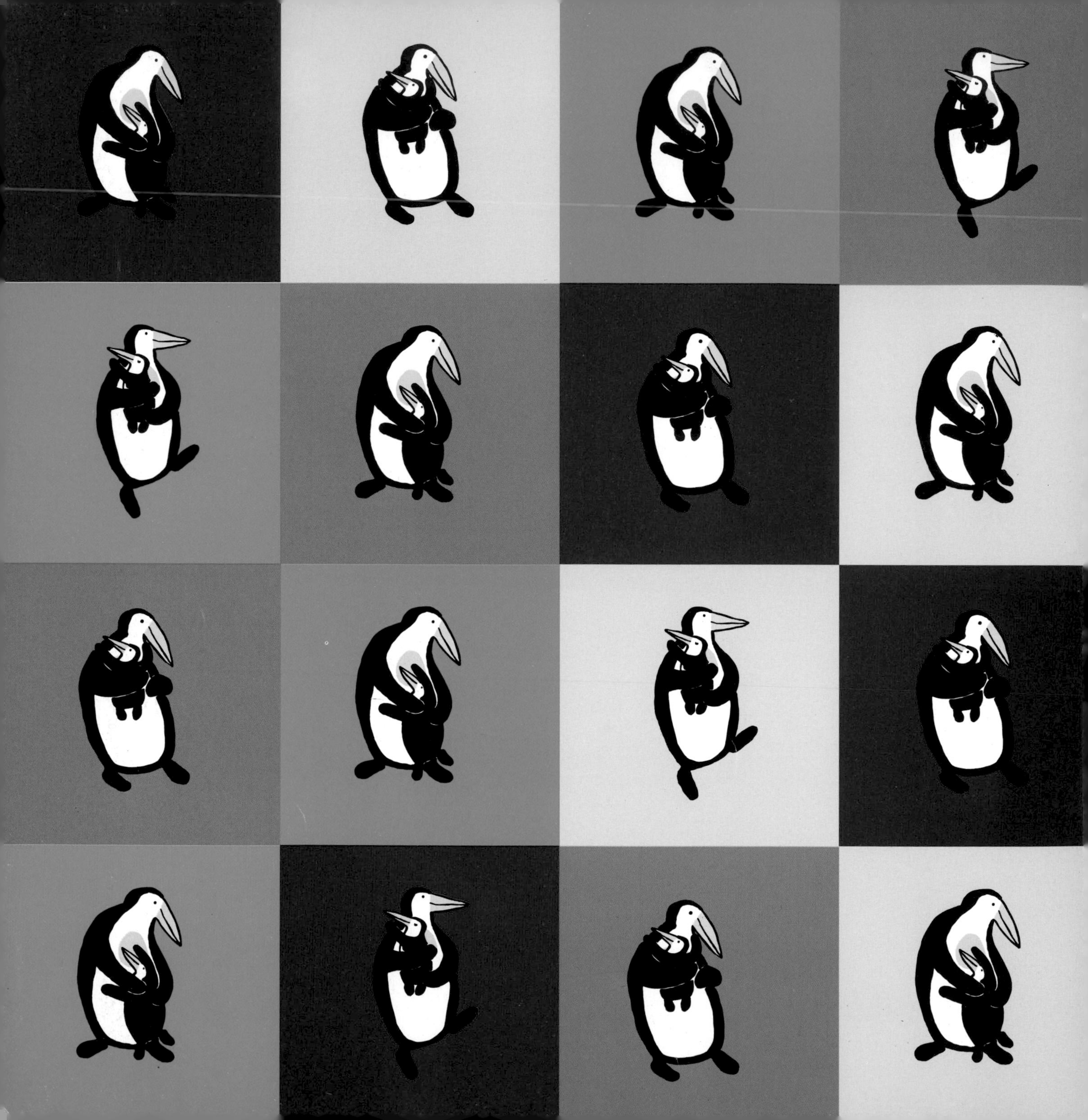

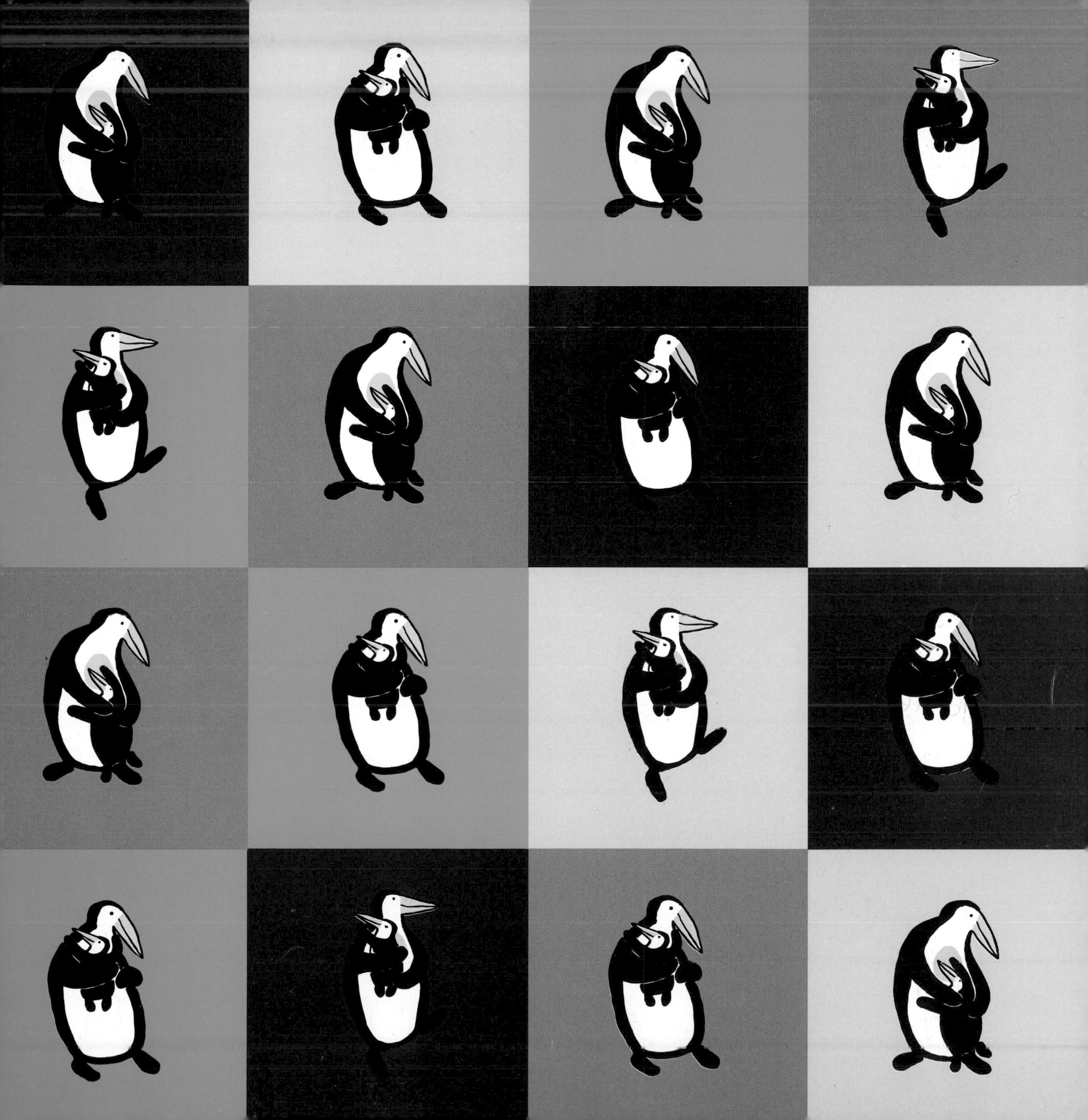

To Brian

First published in Great Britain 1997
by Methuen Children's Books and Mammoth
imprints of Egmont Children's Books Limited
239 Kensington High Street, London, W8 6SL

ISBN 0 7497 3119 2

A CIP catalogue record for this title
is available from the British Library

Printed in Singapore
10

I like it when......

Mary Murphy

I like it
when
you
hold
my
hand

I like it

when

you

let

me

help

Thank you

I like it when we

eat new things

I like it when we

play peekaboo

I like it

when you

tickle

me

you dance with me

I like it
when
you
read
me
stories

I like it when

you hug me tight

I like it when we splash about

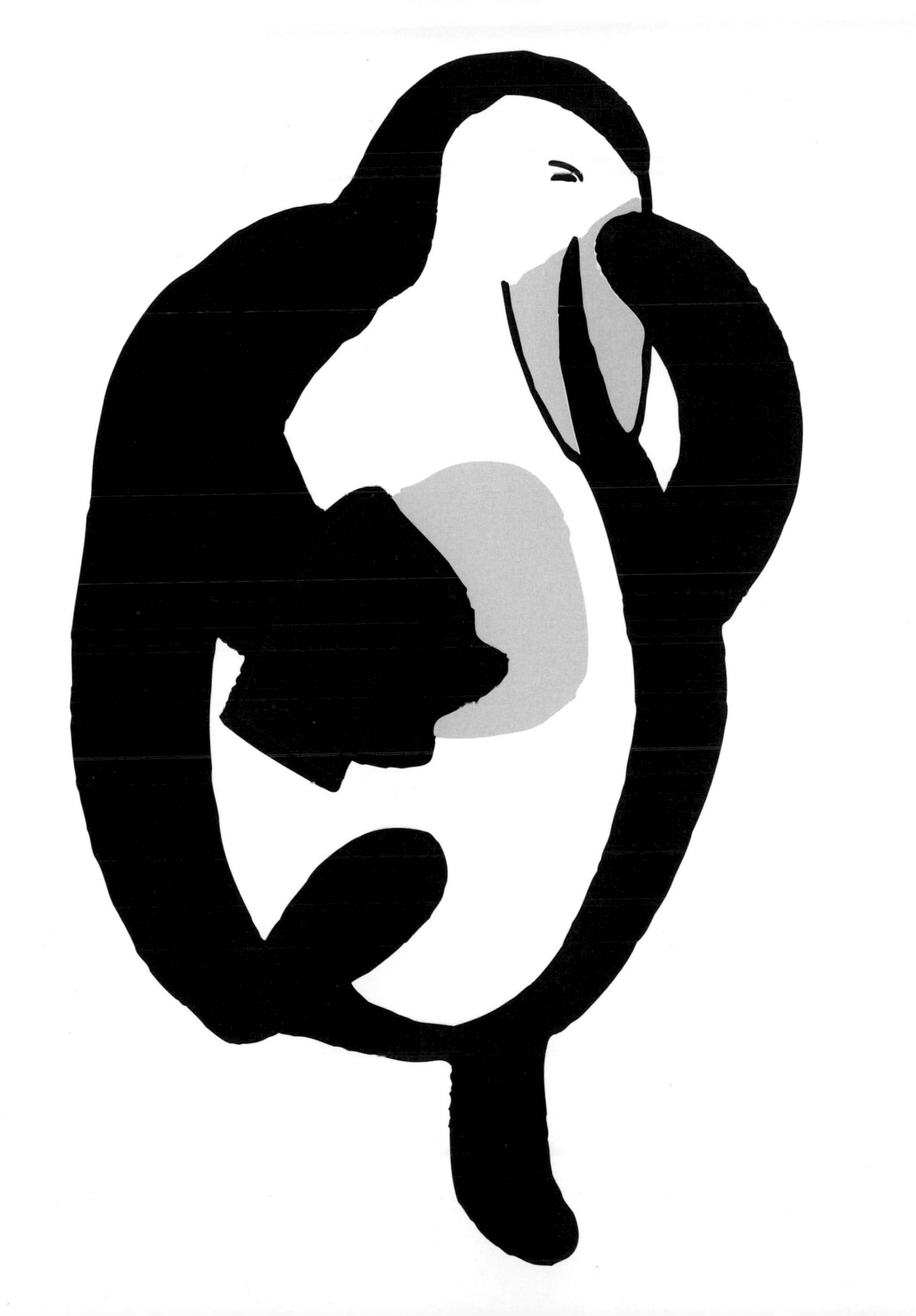

I like it
when
we
kiss
goodnight

Sleeptight
Nightnight

I love you

I love you too

you're wonderful!

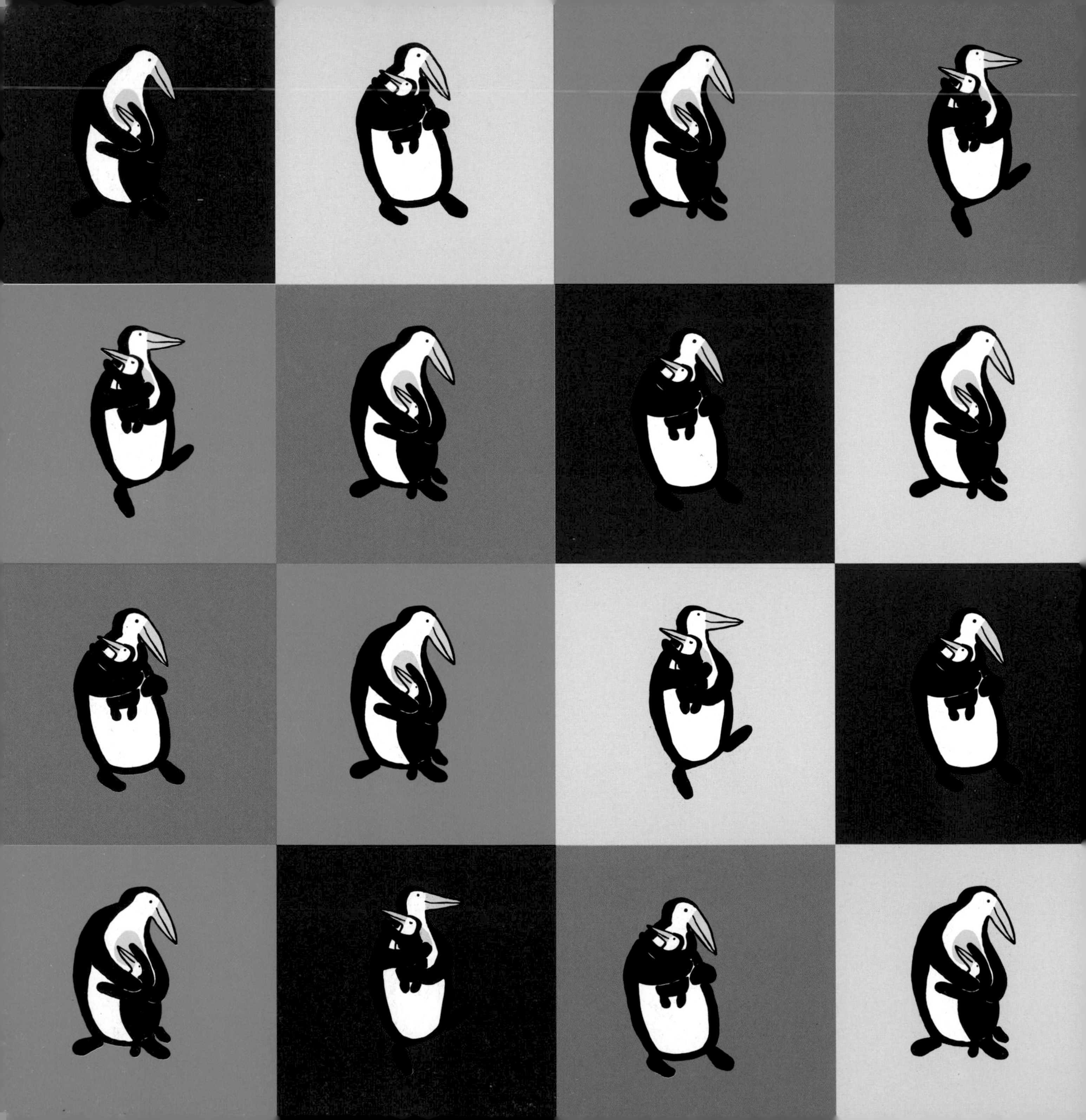

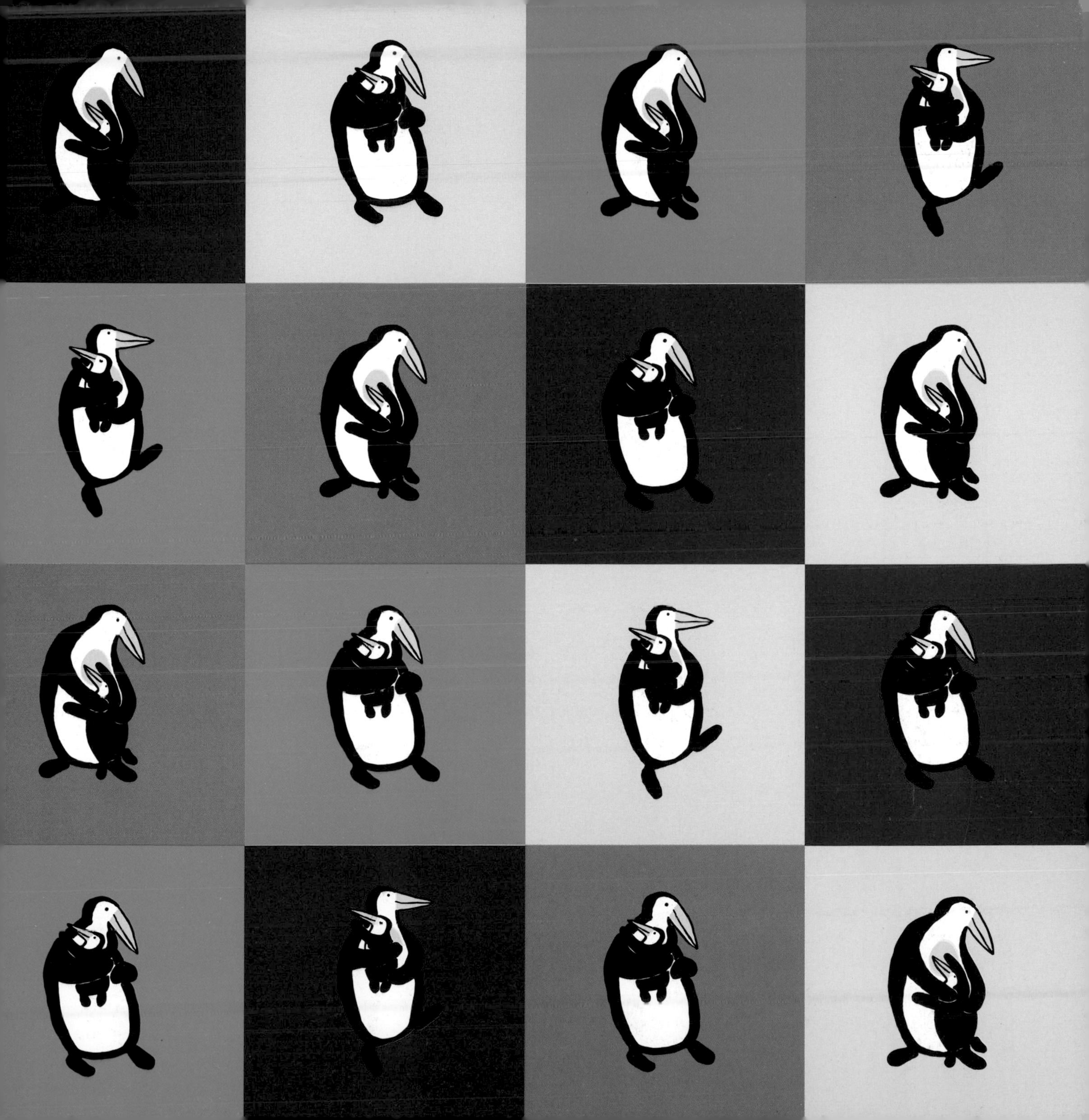

Seven of the Best
Cat's Colours
Jane Cabrera
ISBN 0 7497 3120 6
Do Pigs Have Stripes?
Melanie Walsh
ISBN 0 7497 3026 9
Ella and the Naughty Lion
Russell Ayto and Anne Cottringer
ISBN 0 7497 3019 6
I Like It When
Mary Murphy
ISBN 0 7497 3119 2
When Martha's Away
Bruce Ingman
ISBN 0 7497 2957 0
Mouse Creeps
Reg Cartwright and Peter Harris
ISBN 0 7497 3123 0
Wolf
Sara Fanelli
ISBN 0 7497 2870 1
Picture Mammoth